ZENA and the WITCH CIRCUS

ZENA and the WITCH CIRCUS

by Alice Low
pictures by Laura Cornell

DIAL BOOKS FOR YOUNG READERS

NEW YORK

Dial easy-to-read

For Maggie and her parents with love A.L.

For Lilly and late nights,
and my parents for their help
L.C.

Published by Dial Books for Young Readers
A Division of Penguin Books USA Inc.
375 Hudson Street
New York, New York 10014

Printed in Hong Kong by South China Printing Company (1988) Limited
The Dial Easy-to-Read logo is a registered trademark of
Dial Books for Young Readers, a division of
Penguin Books USA Inc., ® TM 1,162,718.

Library of Congress Cataloging in Publication Data
Low, Alice. Zena and the witch circus / by Alice Low;
pictures by Laura Cornell.
48 p. cm.
Summary: A magically untalented witch is barred from
performing in the Witch Circus until one day
when she becomes a hero.
ISBN 0-8037-0404-6.   ISBN 0-8037-0405-4 (lib. bdg.)
[1. Witches—Fiction. 2. Magic—Fiction.]
I. Cornell, Laura, ill. II. Title.
PZ7.L9595Ze 1990 [E] 87-13567 CIP

First Edition
W
1 3 5 7 9 10 8 6 4 2

The art for each picture consists of an ink, dye,
and gouache painting, which is scanner-separated and
reproduced in red, blue, yellow, and black halftones.

Reading Level 2.1

CONTENTS

THE LAST PRACTICE

Zena loved the School Witch Circus.
Everything about it was magic.

She loved flying in the grand parade
to the tunes of the Wild Witch Band.
She loved fixing up the witch tent
with balloons and shiny paper.
She loved putting on her pink tights,
her purple cape, and her green shoes.

She even liked that funny feeling
in her stomach
as she waited to do her act.
She had that feeling now
in the last practice
before the circus started.

Zena's act was flying
because that was the only magic
she knew how to do.

She wished she could work spells
like the other third-grade witches.
But she was the youngest and smallest
in her class,
and her magic didn't work yet.

Zena felt like a baby.

That's why she *had* to do her act well

and show everyone she was grown-up.

But after practice

Head Witch Hildagrump sent Zena a note:

I fly better than anybody

in our class, Zena thought.

Witch Hildagrump is wrong.

Zena wrote a note to Witch Hildagrump.
She put the note in her crow's beak
and said, "Off you go!"

SAME ACT ONLY MORE SO.
SIX LOOP-THE-LOOPS INSTEAD OF TWO.
TEN FIGURE EIGHTS INSTEAD OF FIVE.
Zena

The crow came back with another note:

Zena started to cry.

"Baby! Baby!" shouted the other
witches in her class.

"I am not a baby," said Zena.

"You'd cry too if you couldn't be
in the circus."

"Well," said Polly, "you should add some *magic* to your flying act. I fly right side up and upside down at the same time. Watch!"

"Nobody can do that," said Zena.

Polly mumbled her spell.

Suddenly there were two Pollys.

"That *is* magic," said Zena.

"I know," said Polly.

"I'm going to win first prize."

Zena started feeling even smaller.

"What's your act?" Zena asked Wog.

"I swim underwater just like a fish."

"Anybody can do that," said Zena.

"*I* never come up for air," said Wog.

Wog mumbled a spell and was gone.

"Where's Wog?" asked Zena.

"Look in the pond," said Polly.

"Wog changed herself into a shark."

"Nobody else can do *that*," said Zena.

"Of course not!" said Wog.

"Those tricks are easy," said Pim.

"I can skate on my broomstick."

"So what!" said Zena. "*That's* easy!"

"Watch!" said Pim.

She mumbled her spell.

Her broomstick stood up straight.

Then Pim skated *up* it!

"You all have great acts," said Zena.

"We know," they all shouted.

"That's why *we're* in the circus."

SOMETHING SCARY

Zena felt very sad.

She needed to be alone to think.

"Gallopazoom!" she said,

and zoomed over the Witch Woods.

She heard some noises: "Arf! Arf!"

Then she saw a cat running.

There was a big dog chasing it.

"Help!" said the cat.

Zena flew down and grabbed it.

She pulled it up behind her.

"How come you can talk?" asked Zena.

"You're not a witch cat."

"One of my friends is a witch cat.

And she taught me how.

My name is Roger. Who arc you?"

"I'm Zena the witch, but I'm not scary.
I can't do any magic."
"Where are you taking me?" said Roger.
"Away from the dragon," said Zena.
"What dragon?" asked Roger.

"The one you were running away from."
"That's not a dragon," said Roger.

"It's a dog. And I'm afraid of dogs."

"Witches call that a dragon,"
said Zena.

"Dragon or dog, it's big and scary,"
said Roger.

"Witches are *really* afraid of dragons,"
said Zena.

"When dragons bark, witches tremble,

and their spells don't work.

But I *love* animals and *I'm* not scared."

Though she was, just a little.

"Wow!" said Roger. "You are brave."

That made Zena feel almost grown-up.

"We've been flying a long time,"

said Roger.

"How long can this thing stay up?"

"Ages. You're safe with me," said Zena.

"We witches are really good at flying."

"Flying with a witch is not
what I call safe," said Roger.

"Would you rather be down there
near the dragon?" asked Zena.

"No!" said Roger. "This is just fine.

Thanks for saving me. You're great!"

That made Zena feel wonderful.

She began to show off

and do tricks on her broomstick.

But she flew too low.

CRASH! They banged into a tree.

IN A FIX

"Ouch!" said Roger. "I bumped my nose. Are you all right?"

"I'm okay," said Zena.

"But my broomstick is broken."

"We have to get away," said Roger.

"Let's fight the dragon," said Zena.

"I'm not fighting that dragon dog with that little stick," said Roger.

"Then let's pretend we're giants," said Zena.

"Pretending won't help," said Roger.

"Then what can we do?" asked Zena.

"You're the witch," said Roger.

"Say a spell to make a real giant
come and scare away the dragon dog."

"But I told you, I can't do spells,"
said Zena. "Anyway, witches' spells
don't work on dragons."

"Because they're afraid of them,"
said Roger. "But *you're* not afraid."
That made Zena tingle all over.
"I'll try," she said.

She thought a while. Then she said:

"Giant, giant, come to me

When I mumble one, two, three.

One, two, three," she mumbled.

It didn't work. No giant came.

31

"WHERE ARE YOU, GIANT?" Zena shouted.

"That's a better voice to use,"

said Roger. "Shout the spell.

When you want a giant to come

you have to use a giant voice.

You can do it."

Zena began to tingle even more.

She shouted:

"GIANT, GIANT, COME TO ME

WHEN I SHOUT OUT ONE, TWO, THREE.

ONE! TWO! THREE!"

The dragon dog stopped barking.

Then it became a giant dragon dog

with giant dragon teeth.

33

It barked louder, like thunder.

The sound made the ground shake,

and the tree shook with it.

SAY THE RIGHT SPELL

"Oh, no!" said Zena.

"I did something all wrong.

I told you I couldn't do magic."

"You *did* magic," said Roger.

"Your spell worked.

It just worked wrong.

You got a giant dragon dog
instead of a giant person."

"I *did* do magic," said Zena.

"I feel really strong."

"Say a spell to mend your broomstick
and get us out of here," Roger begged.

"Good idea!" said Zena. "Here goes:

Broken broomstick near the tree,

Mend when I say one, two, three.

ONE! TWO! THREE!" she shouted.

The pieces of the broomstick

flew up and stuck together.

Then Zena and Roger zoomed away.

"Where are we going now?" asked Roger.

"Back to the circus," said Zena.

"Maybe the other witches can help."

GET RID OF THE DRAGON DOG

Zena and Roger flew to the circus.

The dragon dog followed them inside.

It blocked the doorway and barked

louder than before.

Witch Hildagrump dropped the prizes.

"Help!" shouted the witches.

"Save us!" shouted Witch Hildagrump.

"They can't help you, Zena.

You have to help *them*," said Roger.

"You have to make up a spell
to get rid of the dragon dog."

41

"I don't feel strong enough
to do *that*," said Zena.

"Then make it smaller, like it was."

"But how?" asked Zena.

"Try saying *giant* backward,"
said Roger. "Then maybe
the dragon dog will get smaller."

"Good idea!" said Zena.

"And to make a dragon smaller,

I'll need to use a smaller voice."

"Tnaig, tnaig, magic will be done

When I mumble three, two, one."

When she mumbled "three,"

the giant dragon dog shrank a little.

When she mumbled "two,"

it shrank a little more.

And when she mumbled "one,"

it shrank until it was the size

it had been in the first place.

It barked and jumped,

but it looked very small to Roger.

"I'm not afraid of dogs anymore,"
Roger said.

"Good!" said Zena.

"But the witches are still afraid.

I'd better shrink it one more time."

"*I'd* better go," said Roger.

"My owners will be looking for me.

See you tomorrow."

"Okay," said Zena. "And thanks."

Then she mumbled her spell again,

and the dragon dog became a puppy.

It yipped in a small voice.

"Zena saved us," the witches cried.

"She tamed the dragon and made it tiny."

"Zena the Dragon-tamer wins
first prize," called Witch Hildagrump.

Everybody clapped and clapped.

Zena held her prize in one arm

and the puppy in the other.

"How did you make the dragon become a tame little puppy?" said Wog.

"That's *my* secret magic," said Zena.

"But how will the puppy get along with all our cats?" asked Polly.

"We'll have to see," said Zena.

Then they all flew home.